Emily and the Lamb

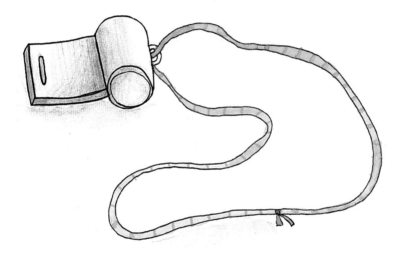

Story by Margaret McAllister
Pictures by Dawn Vince

OXFORD
UNIVERSITY PRESS

Hi, I'm Emily, and I want to tell you about the most brilliant place I know. It's my Gran and Grandad's farm in Scotland, with a stream running past and hills all around it, and animals. I stay there in the school holidays. Gran and Grandad have to get up early to milk the cows even when it's really dark and cold. It's hard work feeding all the animals and keeping them clean, especially in winter. But I go there in summer, and it's great.

There are black and white cows and
calves in the meadow, two horses, lots of
sheep, some chickens, and a black and
white Border collie sheepdog called Jess.
The thing I like best is helping Grandad
with the sheep. My older sisters and cousins
go to the farm too. Sometimes I wish it
could be just me and Gran and Grandad,
and the animals.

My sisters are Katie
and Claire. They talk a lot,
mostly giving me orders. My
cousins are Patrick, Peter, Paul and
Jo. Patrick is really nice. The rest
are OK, but all of them are older
than I am and much bigger. So they
think it's all right to boss
me about.

Katie says I can't carry water to the horses because I can't lift the heavy buckets. OK, so I need two hands and it takes a while and splashes a bit. We can all climb trees, but I sometimes get stuck on the way down, so that Claire says, "Oh, Emily!" and Patrick tries to help, but I don't let him.

We all help with the animals and what I like best is helping Grandad and Jess with the sheep.

One day, we were out on the hill with Jess when Grandad looked up and down and said, "There's a sheep missing. One of the lambs. I'll have to go and find it."

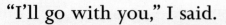

"I'll go with you," I said.

Grandad walked up the hill with great
strides like a long-legged giant. Jess trotted
in front and I hurried behind as fast as I
could, but it's hard to hurry in wellies and
the hill was steep and stony. We climbed
right up to the top of a high, stony ridge
so that we could see for miles. I got out
of breath trying to keep up and my
legs were aching, and we still
hadn't found the lamb.

8

"This will take a long time," said Grandad, and I could guess what was coming next. "And it's going to rain. You don't want to be out on the hill getting soaked right through, do you? What are your cousins doing?"

We looked down. The others were all playing football in the field beside the barn.

"You go and join in," suggested Grandad. "Score a few goals."

"I'd rather stay with you," I said.

"I realize that," said Grandad, "but this lamb could be miles away, and it's all up and down hill. You go and tell Gran there's a lamb missing."

I stomped down the hill and kicked the thistles. Then I kicked a rock and stubbed my toe, and that really hurt. All the way down I looked for the missing lamb. I gave Gran the message, then I asked Patrick if I could join in the football.

"We've already got three on each side," said Katie.
"Emily can be our goalie," said Patrick.

"That's not fair!" said Katie and Claire.

I folded my arms. "It's not fair if I can't play," I said.

"We don't need her," said Paul.

"I'm as good as the rest of you," I said. "I can play for Patrick's team first, then for Katie's team in the second half."

They said that was a silly idea, and Claire laughed at me.

Patrick had a whistle on a string round his neck, and he took it off and gave it to me.

"You can be the referee. That's very important."

"The referee doesn't get to play," I said.

"The referee's the boss," said Patrick. "Just blow your whistle if anybody does anything wrong."

I decided to give it a try. It would be fun bossing them around for a change.

It was a good loud whistle. I stood at the edge of the field and watched carefully so I wouldn't miss anything, especially if Katie cheated. I blew my whistle when Katie ran into Paul and he fell over. I blew it when Jo picked up the ball and threw it. I blew it for anything that didn't look fair. I blew it as hard as I could, but nobody took any notice. They were ignoring the referee! When the ball came towards me, I kicked it to Patrick.

"You can't do that!" shouted Claire. "You're the referee!"

I never wanted to be the referee anyway. Nobody was listening to me.

I went for a walk beside the stream, by myself. I saw a rabbit running across the hill and a speckled fish gliding under the water. The rain began to fall in big, fast drops that made circles on the stream. I turned round to go back to the house, but then I saw something moving.

It was close to the edge, and I ran to get a
better view. The lamb had fallen in the
water up to its neck! The more it kicked,
the more it slipped down into the stream.

"It's all right," I said. "I'll get you out."
Grandad always said you have to be calm
with animals. I lay down on the grass to get
my arms around it. I heaved at the lamb as
hard as I could, but it was no good. It felt as
if it was stuck.

The rain was getting heavier, dripping
through my hair and onto my neck.
I reached further down into the
freezing water to get a better
hold of the lamb, but it was no
use. By that time, the lamb and I
were both so soaked that we
couldn't get any wetter and my
clothes were clinging
to me.

I needed to hold the lamb's head out of the water, so it wouldn't slip back and drown.

I shouted for help, but my voice didn't sound very loud. I wished I could make more noise.

Then I remembered! I still had Patrick's whistle! I hugged the lamb tightly with one arm so it couldn't slip before I got the whistle into my mouth.

"I won't leave you," I said to the lamb. "I'll get you out."

But I knew I couldn't hold on much longer. The rain was pouring down, and the stream seemed to be getting faster. My hands were so cold I couldn't feel them any more. Rain dripped down my face. I could hardly see the poor frightened lamb. I blew again and again! Why didn't anyone come?

Then from far away, I could
hear barking! It was Jess!
I heard Grandad's voice.
"What is it Jess? What's all
that whistling?"
Then Patrick's voice.
"It's Emily! Emily!
Where are you? Are
you all right?"

Grandad arrived, striding down to the stream in his tall boots with Patrick running along the bank. They helped me to pull the lamb out of the water. It was very weak, and its leg was bleeding.

"Will it be all right, Grandad?" I was shivering so much I could hardly get the words out.

Grandad put his old jacket round me and carried the lamb home. I was shivering and soaked to the skin, but I'd saved the lamb. In the farmhouse, we wrapped up the lamb in an old towel and I cuddled it beside the fire to get us both warm. Patrick told Gran what had happened and she brought me some hot chocolate.

Katie and Claire wanted to cuddle the lamb too, but Gran said it had to stay with me. It knew it was safe with me.

22

"You were really brave, Emmy," said
Patrick. "You were soaking wet and
freezing, but you held on to that lamb."

"And it's a good thing you made me the
referee," I said. "That's a really good
whistle!"